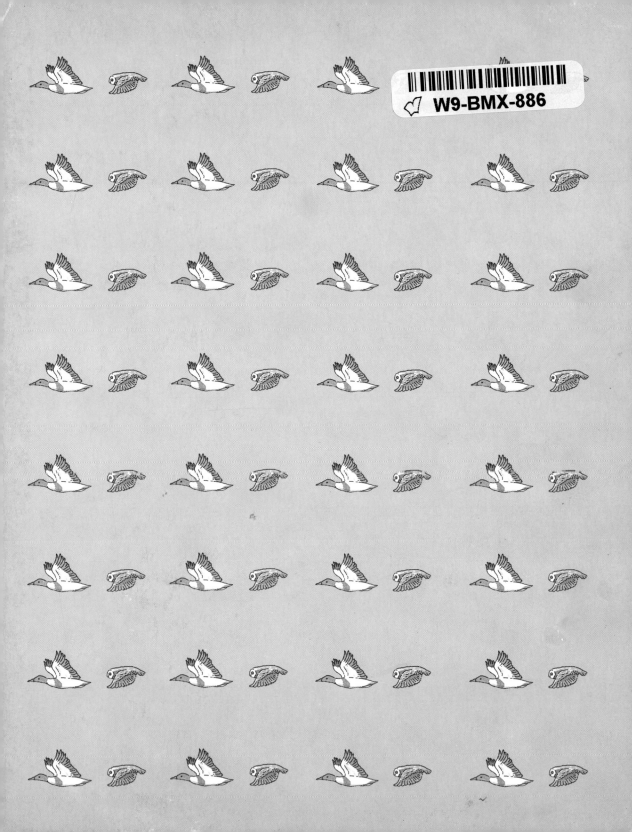

A DORLING KINDERSLEY BOOK

Written by Angela Royston
Photography by Dave King
Additional photography by Cyril Laubscher
(pages 6-7 and 18-19)
Illustrations by Jane Cradock-Watson and Dave Hopkins
Natural History Consultant Steve Parker
Birds supplied by Trevor Smith's Animal World

Aladdin Books
Macmillan Publishing Company
866 Third Avenue
New York, NY 10022

Eye Openers ™
First published in Great Britain in 1992
by Dorling Kindersley Limited,
9 Henrietta Street, London WC2E 8PS

Reproduced by Colourscan, Singapore
Printed and bound in Italy by L.E.G.O., Vicenza

1 2 3 4 5 6 7 8 9 10

Birds.
p.   cm. — (Eye openers)
    "A Dorling Kindersley book" — T.p. verso.
    Summary: Brief text and photographs introduce the sparrow, duck, eagle, parrot, kiwi, flamingo, hummingbird, and owl.
    ISBN 0-689-71644-3
    1. Birds—Juvenile literature. [1. Birds.]
I. Series.
QL676.2.B59   1992
598—dc20   92-8601

·EYE·OPENERS·

Birds

ALADDIN BOOKS
MACMILLAN PUBLISHING COMPANY
NEW YORK

Sparrow

Sparrows build their nests near houses. The mother sparrow lays her eggs and sits on them to keep them warm. After two weeks, the baby birds hatch out. Sparrows eat plant seeds and food from bird feeders, too.

leg

eye

belly

foot

7

Duck

Ducks love swimming on
lakes and ponds. They
use their webbed feet
like paddles to pull
them through the water.
Ducks dip their bills in the
water to feed on snails,
worms, plants, and seeds.

tail

bill

webbed
foot

toe

9

Eagle

This eagle builds its nest on rocky ledges high in the mountains. It glides on its huge wings, hunting for small animals. The eagle swoops down to catch its prey and carry it away in its sharp talons.

wing

head

talons

Parrot

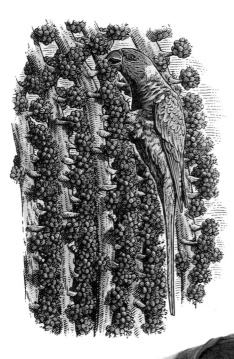

Parrots live together in big flocks. They groom each other with their beaks. For food, they peck at soft fruits and flowers. Some parrots even learn to talk!

head

feathers

beak

Kiwi

Kiwis have tiny wings so
they cannot fly. They build
their nests on the ground
between roots and rocks.
At night, kiwis look for food.
They use their beaks to smell
out bugs and worms to eat.

14

head

leg   whiskers   beak

Flamingo

Flamingos are large pink birds that live by lakes and marshes. They like to wade in shallow water. To find food, flamingos dip their bills upside down and sift through the mud and water.

wing

neck

webbed
foot

bill

Hummingbird

These tiny birds beat their wings so fast they make a humming noise. They feed on flowers. To get their food, they hover near flowers and use their beaks to suck up the juices inside.

beak

wing

feet

Owl

Owls can see and hear well. They eat insects, worms and small mice. They hunt for food at night. As they fly through the woods, they look and listen for their prey and then swoop down to catch them in their talons.

20

eye

talons

tail